Bedtime for Batman is published by
Capstone Young Readers
a Capstone imprint
1710 Roe Crest Drive
North Mankato, Minnesota 56003
www.mycapstone.com

STAR36602

Cataloging-in-Publication Data is available on the
Library of Congress website.

ISBN: 978-1-62370-732-3 (jacketed hardcover)
ISBN: 978-1-62370-733-0 (eBook)

Jacket and book design by Bob Lentz

Printed and bound in the United States of America.
010209R

words by MICHAEL DAHL

pictures by ETHEN BEAVERS

Batman created by BOB KANE with BILL FINGER

BEDTIME FOR BATMAN

CAPSTONE YOUNG READERS
a Capstone imprint

Each day, the sun sets.

Each evening, a dark night rises.

Shadows deepen.

Stars cover
the sky.

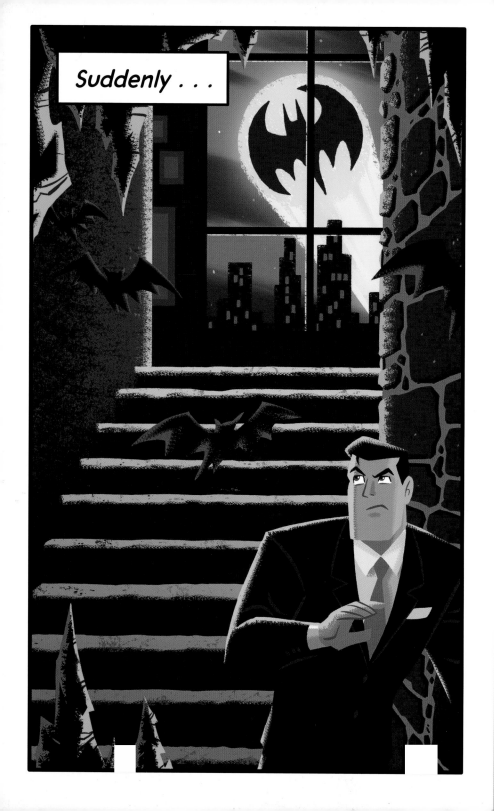

Suddenly . . .

The hero gets a signal.

He must get ready.

Moments later . . .

ZOOM!

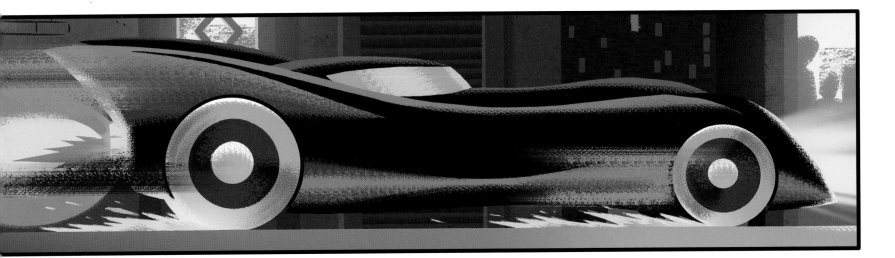

The hero
speeds through
the shadows.

The hero cleans up the daily grime . . .

. . . and brushes aside his fears.

He must
lock away
whatever
he can.

For there are
those who depend
on him.

And those he can count on.

The hero watches
over them all.

He is finally ready . . .

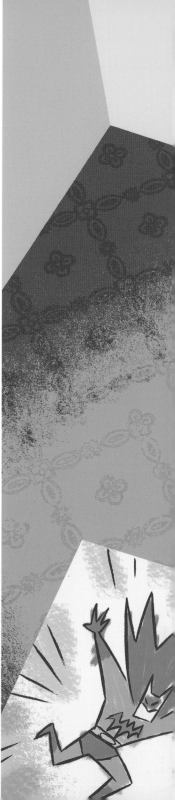

. . . for the long night ahead.

Goodnight, Dark Knight.

BEDTIME CHECKLIST!

Potty

Bath

Pajamas

Teeth

Pick up

Story time